To Hannah

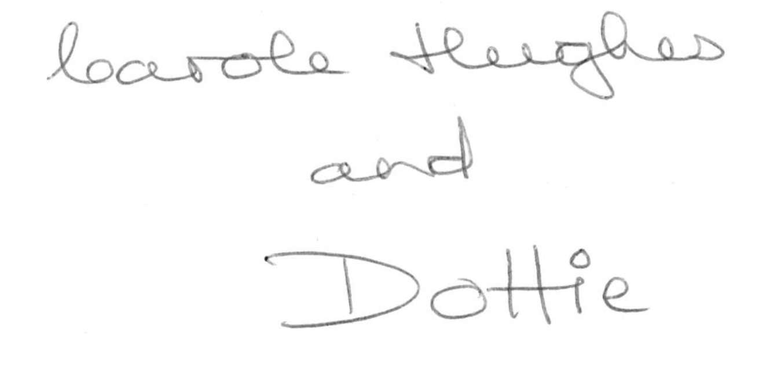

Dec '05.

"Feeling Hot, Hot, Hot!!!"

(Dottie Too)

by
Carole Hughes

authorHOUSE™

1663 Liberty Drive, Suite 200
Bloomington, Indiana 47403
(800) 839-8640
www.AuthorHouse.com

© 2005 Carole Hughes. All Rights Reserved.

No part of this book may be reproduced, stored in a retrieval system, or transmitted by any means without the written permission of the author.

First published by AuthorHouse 11/29/05

ISBN: 1-4208-9514-1 (sc)

Library of Congress Control Number: 2005910233

Printed in the United States of America
Bloomington, Indiana

This book is printed on acid-free paper.

Dottie, the Spottie Dalmatian dog, ready for a new beginning and an even brighter future!

Dedicated to all of Dottie's friends
wherever they may live.

CHAPTER ONE

Dottie awoke with a start, her heart beating like a goat skin drum on Junkanoo Morning. The tangy taste of salt was on her tongue and the stinging scent of silt in her nostrils, she could even hear the sound of waves beating on her ear drums. For one brief moment she was back again, drowning in the horror, fighting for her life. Back again in the nightmare that had nearly taken her life two short months ago. Dottie shook herself vigorously trying to dispel the creeping fear that padded up her spine and chilled her still racing heart. She wondered if she would ever get back to being at peace with the world and everything in it. Somehow, her narrow escape from death at the hands of Hurricane Floyd had undermined the very fundamentals of her existence, and left her a quivering, nervous wreck at every turn. She tried desperately to pull herself together and take stock of her surroundings. She reached out, trying to sense the comforting presence of her Owner, but couldn't detect any movement in the new, and still strange apartment. All that she could hear were the blinds clapping loudly as the strengthening wind disturbed them into motion. The darkness hung heavily around Dottie's shoulders as a vague sense of unease nudged at her consciousness, something was not quite right with the world! It wasn't just the lingering dread of the fading nightmare that was causing the prickling of fear and the raising of hairs along her back, something was definitely amiss! Dottie struggled to her feet, once again shaking herself, trying to shrug off the last vestiges of her dream. She jumped down from the couch. This was only one of the numerous things that had changed in Dottie's life since the Hurricane, one of the few good things! Along with being alive and well and in one piece, she was now officially an Inside Dog. Dottie was not sure who benefited the most from this advent, but both her, and her Owner seemed to glean a great deal of comfort and satisfaction from the new arrangement! Dottie was now allowed, not only to spend the vast majority of her time indoors, lazing luxuriously on the settee, but was also, much to her amazement and delight, welcomed onto her Owner's bed at night! The unspoken agreement had fallen into place almost immediately upon them taking up residence in the New Apartment. In fact it had happened the very first night. Dottie had been sleeping fitfully on the settee, trying to quell the tremors that seemed to plague her whenever night fell. All of a sudden she heard her Owner cry out, the cry seemed to reverberate within Dottie, striking an answering chord in her own soul. In an instant Dottie had bounded up the stairs and hurled herself onto her Owner's bed and into her open arms. The two of them had then spent the night wrapped around each other, each giving sustenance and succour to the other in their mutual hour of need.

From that time on, at any given time of day, Dottie could be found either languishing on the settee or laying claim to the territory that had now become her home. There was no comparison between the home she had lost to that terrible storm surge, and the one that she was now inhabiting. Her old home held memories too terrible to contemplate at present, in the light of its demise. Dottie knew that even her beloved dilly tree, where she had loved to lie and shelter from the noon day sun as it glared down on the rippling creek holding her hypnotised, even it had been swept away in the frantic deluge of the surge. Her new home sported a garden the size of a postage stamp at the back. Truthfully it did overlook the end of one of the channels that guided the boats in from the ocean, but the same sense of space and freedom just wasn't there. In the space of two short months, Dottie had gone from being

Queen of all she surveyed, to being Mistress of a very small manor. Even so, Dottie had marked out her territory with true diligence and now knew every nook and cranny of her domain. This consisted almost entirely of a fenced in square of grass, with a couple of dwarf palms and a small orange tree, as yet in its infancy. Dottie and her Owner lived in the end apartment of a block of four town houses and because they were on the end of the row, their garden was totally flanked on one side by very dense and overgrown bush. This fact in itself had helped Dottie to settle into her new home. When she closed her eyes and listened to all the sounds and movements that emanated from deep within this same area, she could almost imagine that everything had just been a very bad dream from which she would wake up at any moment.

Dottie prowled the house trying to put her paw on what was bothering her. Everything seemed to be in order. Suddenly she felt a tremor which echoed through her whole frame. Lightening flashed razor sharp and blinding, and was followed almost immediately by a long, low rumble of thunder ,that seemed to grumble on and on as though complaining about its role in all of this. The air was alive with electricity, Dottie's sensitive ears could pick up its sounds as it crackled and sizzled across the sky. She realised suddenly that one of the things that was wrong, was the total absence of light and the lack of familiar household noises. The comforting hum of the fans and the groaning of the refrigerator as it reluctantly defrosted itself, these were the sounds that she had become accustomed to during the recent months and it wasn't until they were absent that she noticed them at all. There had been some kind of blackout, Dottie reasoned, and as another jagged flash of lightening scythed across the sky and illuminated the gloomy apartment, she knew with grim certainty that a storm was approaching! A feeling of numb dread invaded her. She knew that she couldn't face another battle with the elements, one had been enough to let her know who was the more powerful! She knew that it had only been sheer luck and grim determination that had pulled her through the ordeal. She did not want to tempt providence with another foray into the fray. As the wind continued to strengthen, the blinds jittered and clacked and the noise rang in Dottie's ears like the applause of a huge audience giving a standing ovation! Then a new sound joined the cacophony, driving rain hammered on the windows and rat-a-tatted on the doors, and to Dottie's horror, began to run down the walls and splatter on the tiles! The force of the rain against the open windows was causing it to splash and puddle on the floor inside! Panic caught in Dottie's throat as she ran upstairs and burrowed under the quilt, if she could just bury herself under enough blankets, she could pretend that all was fine and dandy and nothing to worry about. She lay shaking and whining under the huge quilt as the storm vented its spleen all around her. Suddenly, an image of her father, Delaney, came into her mind, "What on earth are you doing Dottie?" he remonstrated, "you are lying there like a sorry excuse for a dog, thank goodness your mother can't see you now!!" Dottie's face burned with embarrassment, what was she doing indeed? She felt extremely ashamed of herself. She hadn't come this far to spend the rest of her life as a coward. She took a deep breath, threw off the quilt and ran downstairs to survey the damage. Pools of water lay under every window and were getting bigger by the minute! Dottie ran to the linen cupboard and pushed open the door with her nose. She began to pull down towels with her teeth and paws, frantically toppling piles of soft, fluffy towels onto the floor. She then dragged them one by one over to the windows where she positioned them to soak up the water that was already there and to catch the drips as they ran down the walls. In a very short time, Dottie had everything under control, piles of wet towels lay under the windows in every room as the storm wound down to a mumble. Dottie sat down and smiled to herself with satisfaction, and that is exactly how the Owner found her when she came home expecting the apartment to be totally flooded and Dottie a nervous wreck! She fell to her knees and hugged Dottie with gratitude and pride. "Welcome back, you very brave dog." she said as she buried her smiling face in Dottie's neck.

Like an omen, the very next morning, when Dottie pushed her way out into the still wet garden, a double rainbow decked the sky with two perfect arcs of luminous colour. It was a testament to a new beginning and an even brighter future!

CHAPTER TWO

After this breakthrough, somehow everything seemed rosier to Dottie. Life took on a new perspective and a new meaning, and instead of just getting through each day the best she could, she faced every one with a surge of anticipation and excitement. It was as though she had suddenly stumbled upon a land of opportunity and it lay gleaming before her with endless possibility. Dottie lay on her back with her legs stretched up into the air as though trying to reach for something beyond the sky. The sun beat down on her exposed stomach as her paws curled with delight. A soft breeze ruffled her fur and tickled her nostrils, she felt utterly content and at peace. Today she could conquer the world singlehandedly. As she lay soaking up the sun's rays, she heard the chime of the door bell echoing through the apartment. She was immediately on her feet and barking furiously, who dared to disturb her nice little siesta? She ran into the house and stood barking at the front door as the bell chimed again, she pumped up the volume of her barking as the owner came running downstairs to open the door. "Who is it Dottie? Who is it?" asked the Owner and as she opened the door Dottie leapt out almost knocking over the person standing there. As a low growl escaped her lips, Dottie almost fainted with surprise, there stood her Boy surrounded by bags and boxes and a huge grin on his face. Dottie dropped to the floor, a silly grin painted on her lips, not knowing wether to be embarrassed by her mistake or overjoyed by her discovery! She decided on the latter and took to her heels and flew in circles around him, skidding to a halt only to take off again. Her heart felt as though it would explode with joy, and when she finally came to a standstill in front of him, he bent down to hug her and fondle her silky ears."Have you missed me Dottie?" he said through his laughter. Oh, what a wonderful place the world is when you are loved unconditionally and without exception! As the Boy and the Owner busied themselves carrying the bags and boxes inside, Dottie investigated all the strange and foreign smells that clung like parasites to the Boys things.

The next few days flew by in a flurry of activity. Everywhere the Boy went, Dottie was his shadow. She couldn't risk letting him out of her sight for one second, in case he disappeared from her life again. So many terrible things had taken place since he had last left them, that subconsciously she associated his absence with bad luck and misfortune. Consequently she dogged his every footstep with grim determination.

One morning bright and early, just as the sun was raising its radiant face to the world, the Boy called Dottie's name and together they descended the rickety wooden staircase that led down to their dock. Dottie's tail wagged wildly, slapping a rhythm against the wooden rails as they went down. The Boy's little skiff had not survived the Hurricane but had been totally smashed to pieces by the vengeful storm. Dottie wondered what kind of seaworthy craft the Boy had managed to get his hands on. She knew that like her, the Boy could not be content for long to be a "landlubber".She knew that eventually the irresistible call of the sea would get the better of him, and he would succumb to the urge to be a part of that aqua vastness that they both so loved. Tied to the dock was the strangest contraption that Dottie had ever laid eyes on. To her experienced eye it looked like a cross between a boat and a motor cycle. The boat part was small and streamlined with turquoise and purple speed stripes painted along its pointed hull. Then, there seemed to be a motor cycle seat and handlebars perched on the top, most peculiar! Dottie was used to leaping into the nice sturdy stern of a boat, where she would sit and watch the receding land while the water churned and foamed in a jet stream behind them. She loved to feel the cool, refreshing water spraying over her. She couldn't quite make out where she was

He had an arm on either side of her as he gripped the handlebars, this gave her a limited amount of stability, like restraining straps or safety belts, holding her in position.

supposed to sit on this monstrosity. The Boy put his belongings into a compartment under the seat and motioned for Dottie to join him, as he straddled the vehicle as though he were about to ride a horse. He indicated for Dottie to jump onto the space in front of him. As far as she could make out it was just a narrow ledge of saddle that she was supposed to sit on and it looked extremely unsafe to her. However, Dottie was still the adventuress at heart and this certainly was a whole new experience. She was not about to fail her Boy, so she cast her fate to the wind and jumped. Dottie's feet slithered and slipped as she tried to gain her equilibrium. The vessel bucked and lurched on impact and the Boy held on to her for dear life, as the two of them nearly capsized. Eventually, everything calmed down and Dottie regained her footing and perched precariously on the seat in front of the Boy. He had an arm on either side of her as he gripped the handlebars, this gave her a limited amount of stability, like restraining straps or safety belts, holding her in position. The Boy revved up the engine and in a cloud of smoke, the vehicle lurched forward and took off for the open sea, spewing a jet of sea water behind it. Dottie's feet kept sliding away from her as the seat vibrated beneath her. She concentrated on keeping a grip as the wind flapped her ears around her head and the stinging salt spray blurred her vision. The Boy was driving the contraption faster and faster into the wind and he was whooping with joy as he went. A sense of elation invaded Dottie as she responded to his mood. This was what life was all about, freedom and joy, adventure and living to the fullest measure every single day. They swerved and zigzagged and did circles, as the sun smiled down on them from a cloudless sky. "Better be heading back now," said the Boy as he did one last skid in the water and laughed uproariously as a wall of water totally engulfed them both. Soon they were back at their dock and Dottie jumped to safety and stability once more. Her legs trembled with exertion as she made her way back up the steps to her very own back yard. The Owner was sitting in the shade reading as Dottie approached, "How did you like the jet ski Dottie?" she asked. So that's what it was, a jet ski, no less! Dottie made a bee line to the bowl of fresh water that was waiting for her and completely submerging her face in it, she gulped it down greedily. Jet skiing was certainly very thirsty work!

CHAPTER THREE

The household was a hive of industry, the Boy had carried in a huge tree and placed it in a bucket of heavy stones. It stood in a corner of the room, tall and straight like a sentry, watching over them all. The Owner kept bringing down box after box from the attic and putting them in a pile on the living room floor. Dottie was intrigued, what on earth was going on? She monitored every movement from her position on the settee, her head bobbing up and down as though it were on a spring. Finally, the Owner started tearing open boxes and the Boy joined her efforts. Soon there were all kinds of shiny baubles, ornaments and knick knacks strewn all over the floor, long ribbons of glittery stuff lay tangled in a heap, and as the Boy fiddled with something behind the tree, the whole room was suddenly illuminated by multicoloured specks of twinkling light. Dottie could not believe her eyes as she gazed in awe at the rainbow of coloured lights that dazzled her sight. Then the Owner began to hand each treasure to the Boy, who very carefully placed them onto the branches of the tree. Soon the entire tree was ablaze with shimmering colours and sparkling lights. As its glory radiated out into the room, the Boy and the Owner joined Dottie on the settee, and they sat, like the three Magi, lost in wonder and adoration. The Boy was the first to speak, "Isn't it beautiful?" he gasped, "Now it really feels like Christmas!"

The days that followed seemed to be full of excitement for Dottie. All kinds of packages and parcels appeared under the tree and Dottie sneezed mightily as she sniffed and snuffled at the shiny bows and silken tassels. The Boy was constantly running off on errands and sometimes he would take Dottie with him. She would sit patiently in the car while he shopped for items for the Owner, or accompanied him on her leash when he went to visit friends. She would lie drowsily napping in the shade while he tinkered with various projects, his friends standing around giving advice and enthusiastically bringing him up to date on all that had transpired in his absence.

One day the house was even busier than usual, the door bell chiming with annoying regularity and people coming and going with delicious and enticing smelling pots and dishes. Dottie retired to the back yard and lay under the palm tree, where she could have a certain amount of peace, if not quiet. Everyone was so busy, and she just kept getting under their feet. It was better to just keep totally out of the way, she reasoned. Things seemed to quieten down as the day wore on, and so she decided to venture inside to see what all the fuss had been about. The apartment had undergone a transformation! All the furniture had been pushed back against the walls, the dining room table was draped with a brightly coloured cloth, and candles were flickering merrily along its length. Coloured lights hung from everywhere, twinkling like stars on a cold winter's night. Mouth watering smells emanated from the kitchen, and the air was redolent with a sense of gaiety and expectation. "There you are Dottie!" said the Owner, emerging from the kitchen, her face glowing pink and her hair clinging damply to her head. She was wiping her hands on a towel as she spoke, she turned to the Boy,"Spruce Dottie up a bit for the party would you? The guests will be here soon." The Boy took Dottie back outside and began to brush her coat with long, firm strokes, she closed her eyes and lost herself in the sensation. She felt tingly and warm all over. She smiled to herself, she loved parties! Inevitably at some point she always became the centre of attention, and she just loved every moment of it! The Boy tied a red ribbon around her neck and as she moved, a silver bell tinkled at her throat." You look like one of Santa's helpers," he chortled as he returned inside with Dottie at his heels.

Soon guests began to arrive with much chatter, goodwill and laughter! In no time at all the small apartment was full to the brim and overflowing with noisy, happy people. Dottie did the rounds until her appetite for love and admiration became satiated for the time being. She made her escape upstairs to the relative sanity of the bedroom. She settled down on the soft quilt and tried to nap. After a while she gave up trying to get some sleep, the thrum of the music and tinkle of laughter were too distracting, and so with a resigned," if you can't beat them join them" attitude, she padded downstairs to join the happy throng. The crowd had dwindled somewhat and many of the guests were sitting around in groups talking animatedly. As Dottie made her rounds once more, she noticed that there were quite a few carelessly discarded plates and glasses scattered around the apartment, on the floor and on the low tables that dotted the room. She decided to investigate ,and much to her delight and satisfaction discovered that many held juicy morsels of food and treats, which she consumed immediately.

When she sniffed in the glasses, she found a whole new spectrum of scents. Some held sweet, fruity aromas, some tickled her nose with fizzy bubbles, others had strong, eye watering chemical odours, but best of all were the ones that held milky, sweet, coconutty ones! These she decided to try, and was soon searching around for more glasses containing the delicious nutty liquid. Each time she found what she was looking for, she placed her nose inside the glass and sucked up the rich contents! Before too long she began to feel a warmth spreading through her which radiated out from her stomach to the very tips of her ears, tail and every single toe! Dottie continued on her quest for the delicious, milky treat, and managed to find two more glasses with the very same liquid in them. One of the glasses was half full and Dottie lay down with it held firmly between her front paws and slurping noisily, she consumed every drop! Suddenly the Owner's voice rang out in alarm," Dottie! No! That's alcohol, you silly dog! Oh, my goodness she's just drunk coconut rum and milk!" Everyone's attention was on Dottie, as the room grew quiet. Dottie looked guiltily around, not quite knowing exactly what it was that she had done. It was then that she noticed that the room seemed to be moving around of its own accord, and that the people who were staring at her, had two faces each! There was also a dreadful buzzing in her ears that drowned out most of what was being said to her. She began to feel extremely uncomfortable and thought it best if she just went to lie down. However, when she tried to find the stairs, her legs seemed to get away from her and she bumped painfully into the wall! She just could not get her bearings and with a nervous whimper, she sat down heavily and felt herself swaying like a palm tree in the breeze! Finally, amid much laughter, the Boy came to her rescue, and picking her up bodily in his arms, carried her upstairs and laid her gently on the bed. "You crazy girl," he said to her,"tomorrow you are going to feel awful, you won't be doing that again in a hurry!" and with that, he kissed the top of her head and left her to her confusing and troubled dreams.

Each time she found what she was looking for, she placed her nose inside the glass and sucked up the rich contents!

CHAPTER FOUR

Dottie awoke to the sound of cleaning up operations downstairs. She could hear the Boy and the Owner working together cheerfully to put the apartment back to its former state. She stretched lazily, actually she felt quite good for saying. Her head felt as though she were wearing one of those sporty headbands and her stomach roiled greasily when she moved, but otherwise there was nothing that a good run in the fresh air wouldn't fix. She jumped off the bed and padded downstairs to see what was going on. The Boy and the Owner had just about finished getting the place back to normal and greeted Dottie happily. "Do you want to go to the beach?" the Boy asked her. Did she indeed! She ran to the front door, tail wagging frantically and yelping with anticipation. The Boy could hardly get her leash clipped onto her collar, she was so excited. They set off for the beach, which was only about a ten minute walk away. Dottie kept to the side of the road where she could investigate the myriad smells, of people and animals that had passed this way before them. It was good to be out and about with her Boy keeping her company. Dottie felt the blood pumping through her veins as she trotted along and was content and happy. When they reached the beach, they saw several fishermen sitting on the quay, line fishing. They were baiting their hooks with chunks of raw conch and then casting their lines with a flourish. So far the buckets were empty, but it was early yet and they were seasoned fishermen, so it was only a matter of time and patience before the fish started biting.

Dottie and the Boy surveyed the beach, the salty air stung their nostrils as they breathed deeply, filling their lungs with the pure, sweet air. Their eyes took in the vast turquoise blue carpet of ocean that unfurled in front of them, dazzling them with its beauty. Their feet began to sink into the powdery, white sand that stretched endlessly, and without flaw on either side of them. In a flash of mutual decision, Dottie and the Boy, as though one entity, began to run, their feet kicking up showers of white sand behind them. They ran ,mouths wide open, legs pumping like pistons, the Boy letting out a shrill cry of elation and Dottie echoing it with a resounding bark. They ran until the Boy fell in a heap on the ground gasping for breath, and Dottie slowed to a halt beside him. They lay there together, gazing at the heavens and wallowing in their splendour. Reluctantly, the Boy pulled himself to his feet with a sigh, "I miss all of this," he said, indicating his surroundings with a sweep of his arm, "I hate the cloying claustrophobia of city life Dottie, I can't wait to finish college and come home." Dottie put her head on one side and voiced her agreement with a whine. "Let's GO!" he yelled as he took off full pelt in the opposite direction, heading for home. Dottie sped off, catching up and overtaking him in a matter of seconds. The fishermen waved their farewells as the Boy and the Dog flew past in a shower of sand.

When they reached the apartment, the Owner greeted them with, "Baths, both of you, you look like a pair of sand monsters!" The Boy took off upstairs towards the shower, and Dottie slunk around the back of the house. She had spotted the Owner unrolling the long, green hosepipe, that lay coiled on the front path. She absolutely hated baths, which was strange really, because she absolutely loved swimming in any body of water that she could find. Somehow to her, baths seemed a little undignified, having someone scrubbing away at your most intimate parts and under your armpits, was most unladylike and to be avoided at all cost! She took one look at the unfurling hose pipe and quickly disappeared from sight. She plopped down under the palm tree and pretended that she had no idea what was going on. She lay there for quite some time, in fact she really began to think that she had escaped the indignity, until the Owner rounded the corner, brandishing a scrubbing brush in one hand and a big bottle of doggie shampoo in the other! She had a very determined look on her face, and Dottie knew from experience that there was little or no point in resisting. She surrendered herself to the onslaught, and was actually quite surprised to discover that it was not half as bad as she had envisaged and actually turned out to be quite a pleasant interlude. She did feel hot and sandy and the cool water and gentle scrubbing motion felt therapeutic on her skin. Soon she was done and the final rinse had washed away any remaining sand. The Owner rubbed her down with her very own towel [it was red and blue with the sweetest Dalmatian family depicted on it.] She was finished! She had a quick race around the property to get rid of any last vestiges of water, and then she was ready for a nice afternoon nap in the shade of the palm tree. She flopped down and closed her eyes, in an instant she was snoring softly, her lips vibrating with the sound.

She absolutely loved swimming in any body of water that she could find.

CHAPTER FIVE

All too soon the idyllic, fun filled days came to an end, as all vacations must, even if you do live in the Bahamas! It was time for the Boy to return to college for the next semester, and he would not be back again for another six months. To Dottie the time meant nothing, her concept of time was not governed by the ticking of a clock, but by some internal time keeper that informed her of the passage of time. This was directly related to her needs and desires. For example, she always knew when the

Owner was due to return from work each day, and began to fret if she didn't appear within the time frame. She also knew when it was dinner time, not only by the grumbling of her stomach, but also because she had become used to a routine and this was an important part of it. She knew that the sun rose and set each day with the regularity of clockwork, and that life went on regardless of who came or went in your life. She would miss the Boy terribly, just as she had once more become used to him being there, he was going to go off and leave her again. A terrible sense of sadness and loss invaded her spirit as she watched his bags and boxes being loaded into the car, and as he turned to give her one last wave, she felt as though part of her was leaving too, part of her was Miami bound.

The house was so quiet and empty when he had gone. Not a whisper of noise disturbed the eerie stillness. She walked outside, even the wind sighed as it rustled through the palm trees. The sound of the water lapping against the dock seemed muted somehow, as though she were in a surrealistic world, a mirror image of real life. The centre of her universe had been snatched away and she was left with just the shell, a brittle facade that she must nurture carefully until he returned to take his rightful place at the centre of her world.

When the Owner returned from the airport alone, the two of them sat, side by side on the front doorstep looking out over the tree tops, as though charting his progress through the skies, tugging their hearts behind him.

Much later that evening, Dottie and the Owner sat on the settee sharing a bowl of nuts, Dottie's favourite treat. She lay with her head on the Owner's lap enjoying the snacks and the closeness of someone who loved her. There was a film on television and as it flickered and droned, Dottie felt herself drifting into the Land of Nod with never a thought of loneliness or desertion!

CHAPTER SIX

Normally Dottie would sleep all night through, only opening her eyes as the shards of sunlight forced their way through the blinds and the birds' songs became too loud to ignore. However, this particular night, Dottie suddenly found herself wide awake and her hackles up. She wasn't quite sure what it was that had disturbed her, but whatever it was, had her adrenaline pumping! As Dottie sniffed the air, she detected a scent she was not familiar with, but which seemed to stir something deep inside her, something feral that had long been dormant in her species. Dottie carefully got to her feet, soundlessly jumped off the bed, and stealthily began to prowl through the apartment. It was then that she heard it, a faint squeaking sound accompanied by the patter of very tiny feet. The noises were coming from the attic, and as Dottie listened, she could make out that there were at least two of the intruders and they were running backwards and forwards in the roof. Something kept Dottie from barking then and there, some second sense that made her keep perfectly still with ears pricked. After a few minutes, she detected gnawing noises around the hatch at the top of the stairs. Soon a gentle shower of sawdust started to fall, glittering like golden rain in the moonlight. Dottie still sat, head on one side quizzically. Soon a little hole began to appear in the hatch and Dottie could make out two sets of razor sharp teeth, hard at work. Her fur bristled with loathing and a menacing growl escaped her lips. The gnawing ceased immediately and four beady eyes glinted from the hole, Dottie's blood ran cold as she perceived these evil creatures staring at her. She began to bark at them with all the hatred she could muster, and it was considerable. Her whole body shook with the force of her effort. The Owner came running out of her bed in fright, switching on lights as she ran. When she followed Dottie's gaze and saw the hole in the hatch, she gasped in horror, "RATS!!" she said with disgust.

After that no-one got any sleep, the Landlord was summoned, and every light in the house turned on. Dottie ran from room to room grumbling and muttering incessantly, her nose in the air ,ready to catch any scent of rodent. So far they seemed to be contained in the roof, fortunately Dottie had sensed them before they had managed to invade the interior of the apartment. The Landlord was outside with a huge torch trying to determine how they had got in the roof in the first place. Eventually he dragged a ladder into the yard and leant it against the wall of the apartment. He pointed out a large jagged hole, next to the airconditioning pipes where they entered the roof, under the eaves. He went back to his own apartment and returned carrying chicken wire and cement mix. By the light of the torch, which he held clamped under his chin, he covered the hole with a piece of chicken wire and cemented it in place. "That should stop any more from coming in." he said smugly,"Now to deal with the happy couple we have inside!"

Dottie had taken up her position as sentry under the hole inside, and glared fixedly at it, as she sat rigidly to attention at the top of the stairs. A low growl vibrated through her frozen frame every time she sensed any kind of movement from above. When the Landlord finally made his way up the stairs to join her, her tail wagged appreciatively from side to side. "We need to put some rat poison in the roof, and then seal up that hole." advised the Landlord, dragging the ladder up the stairs behind him and wedging it precariously on the landing. Dottie jumped to her feet, ears perked, tail stiff as a board as he ascended to the hatch, clutching a bag of rat poison in one hand and holding tightly to the ladder with the other. As he reached the top step and stretched up to push the hatch door to one side, there was a scrabbling, scrambling sound above him. Two sleek, black bodies with long, pink tails, leapt from the hole and landed with a thud on the staircase behind him! Dottie nearly jumped out of her skin! The moment she had been waiting for had arrived, a chance to come to grips with the interlopers once and for all! She fairly flew down the stairs, briefly making contact with each step as she raced after them. The Owner was standing at the foot of the stairs and as the creatures ran over her feet, she began to jump up and down and scream for all she was worth! This spurred Dottie on even more, the fact that they had had the audacity to frighten her Owner was more than she could bear! She was even more determined to run them to earth.

The rats split up, one diving into the kitchen and disappearing behind the fridge, the other making a beeline for the laundry room and scampering under the washing

She fairly flew down the stairs,
briefly making contact with each
step as she raced after them.

machine. Dottie skid to a halt in the middle of the dining room. She was frustrated, she could smell them so strongly and yet could not get at them, so near and yet so far! She barked and whined as she ran from one place to the other, her nose grazing the ground as she went. Then the Owner grabbed a broom and said to Dottie, "Let's get them girl, let's get the rats!!" and she began banging on the side of the washing machine with the broom. As the noise echoed through the apartment, the rat zipped out from its hiding place straight in front of Dottie, who had been waiting expectantly. Dottie pounced and caught the rat between her teeth and began to shake her head vigorously. The Owner opened the patio door and Dottie ran outside with the rat still held firmly in her mouth. It was squeaking loudly and struggling to free itself, but Dottie kept a tight hold on it until she reached the dock, where with a flourish she sent it flying through the air. It landed with a splash in the water and within seconds was swimming, for dear life, out to sea. Dottie monitored its progress with satisfaction, she doubted that it would be coming back this way anytime soon!

She hurried back inside, still ready for action. The Owner had managed to corner the other rat in the kitchen, and as Dottie entered, it shot past her and was making its way to the patio door. Dottie was soon in hot pursuit, and as it streaked outside into the garden, she was close behind. It ran in a zig zag pattern, trying to shake her off, and finally disappeared under the fence into the bush. Dottie sat by the fence, panting loudly and grinning from ear to ear. She had sent both rats on their way and neither would be in too much of a hurry to return. She felt good, she had honoured her obligation to protect both her Owner and her property, and had also had great fun doing it!

As Dottie looked around, she realised that it was already morning and that the sun was struggling onto the horizon with its huge, shining face smiling at her. Life was wonderful, she thought, as she trotted inside to see what was for breakfast.

Dottie went straight to the spot where they had encountered the puppies the day before.

CHAPTER SEVEN

Spring was always a pleasant season in the Bahamas, with comfortably warm temperatures and cooling breezes redolent with Honeysuckle, Frangipani, Bougainvillea and Jasmine. Everything seemed fresh and new with a lushness only possible in sub-tropical climes.

Dottie lay under her palm tree watching a Humming bird, as its long beak pierced the centre of a Hibiscus flower and its tiny wings vibrated, filling the air with a hypnotic thrumming. A Dragonfly zoomed by, its iridescent, gossamer wings looking too frail to keep its large body air bourne. Under the eaves of the apartment Hornets were noisily constructing their nest, buzzing busily to and fro as the cratered construction rapidly took shape. An Egret swooped to a standstill almost under Dottie's nose, its long, twig like legs bending as it landed. Dottie barked a warning at it, she didn't quite know what she would do if it turned on her, but she felt it her duty to warn it anyway. The regal, Heron like bird strutted around the yard for a while, preening its snow white plumage, perching precariously on one leg as its tiny head darted backwards and forwards. Then, as quickly as it had come, it departed, with a whoosh of air, it soared heavenwards and soon was a mere dot in the clear blue sky.

Dottie felt antsy, all day she had been experiencing what she could only describe as "the jitters." A feeling of expectation fluttered in her breast and her paws tingled as though already on the road to new adventures! She jumped to her feet and stretched, placing her head between her front paws on the ground and her rear end high in the air, tail pointing skywards as straight as an arrow! She investigated the perimeters of the yard, carefully sniffing every inch, determined to root out any new or unusual scents. As she neared the side of the yard that bordered the area of bush, her nose picked up a new, but familiar scent. She focussed all her attention on the smell, it was a distinctly canine odour and it was coming from somewhere deep within the bush. Dottie began to whimper and scratch at the base of the fence. Soon she was barking loudly, in fact so loudly, that the Owner came outside to see what all the fuss was about. Dottie continued to burrow furiously, as though determined to dig an escape route under the fence! "Stop it Dottie," the Owner said angrily, "You're going to ruin the fence. What on earth is the matter?" As Dottie continued with her quest, the Owner grasped her firmly by her collar and pulled her sharply away. "Let's go and see what's bothering you," she said, urging Dottie inside and clipping on her leash. They then went out of the front door and followed the path that led into the bush. Dottie immediately picked up the scent and was soon surging ahead with the Owner being pulled forward, clutching onto the leash. Dottie's tail rotated in complete circles as the scent increased in strength, now she could hear whimpering and short, sharp yapping sounds. Within seconds they came upon four tiny puppies, partially hidden in the undergrowth. Dottie immediately began alternately licking and sniffing the tiny creatures as they wriggled and squeaked under her administrations. One of them, a little brown puppy with a black nose and ears, was trying to keep out of her way and growled and snapped at her as it teetered on shaky legs. This amused Dottie , such an aggressive little thing with so much courage! Dottie and the Owner decided that it was best to leave the puppies where they were, as surely the mother would be returning anytime soon. The Owner deliberately had not touched them, as she knew that to put her scent on them would immediately seal their doom. They were obviously the offspring of one of the many bush dogs that roamed the island in packs, keeping out of the way of humans and the ever increasing flow of traffic. These 'Potcakes', as these mixed breed dogs were called, were often dogs who had originally been mistreated or abandoned by their owner and had learned to survive in the wild.

That night Dottie slept very fitfully, glimmers of dreams haunted her dozes and woke her in fits and starts. The recurring theme of her visions seemed to be abandoned puppies.

CHAPTER EIGHT

The next morning Dottie was up and about very early and went straight to the fence to sniff the air inquisitively. To her surprise she saw that one of the puppies had found its way to the fence and was lying rolled up in a tight furry ball at the base. Dottie nudged it through a gap in the fence with her cold, wet nose. It gave a weak but meaningful growl and bared its tiny teeth in a grimace. Dottie realised that it was the very same little hero from the day before! Somehow he had managed to make his way to Dottie's apartment and was now lying totally wiped out by the sheer effort of it all! His little sides rose and fell as he panted with exhaustion, and his tiny, pink tongue lolled as he gasped for water. Dottie was suddenly very worried, she could sense that the puppy was literally on his last legs and that if she didn't do something soon, it could be too late! She ran inside the apartment and took to the stairs with a flying leap. She fairly exploded into the Owner's bedroom, waking her with insistent barks. The Owner followed her downstairs and outside to the fence, where Dottie frantically jumped up and down with impatience. When the Owner saw the puppy, she said,"Oh, the poor little thing!" and quickly went inside to get a box and a towel. Together they went into the bush to retrieve the puppy. As the Owner tried to place the towel over it to lift it up, he valiantly snapped at her hands in defence. Eventually they managed to get the little creature into the box and carefully placed it near the fence. Then they went into the bush to find out what had happened to the other puppies. Dottie went straight to the spot where they had encountered the puppies the day before. There was no sign of any of them, and even though they searched in ever increasing circles, they found no trace of the little family. The Owner decided that it would be a good idea to concentrate on the one puppy that they had found, so they made their way to the box where the little creature lay motionless. The Owner gently touched his face with one finger, and much to her relief, the tiny mouth opened in a half hearted growl.

When they got back to the apartment, the Owner called the Humane Society and within minutes the little patient was on his way to the healing and expert hands of the local Veterinarian. During the whole of this procedure, Dottie stood guard over the cardboard box, never flinching or allowing her attention to be distracted from the job in hand. After all,it was her who had found the puppies in the first place and it was an undisputable fact that she was solely responsible for saving the life of "Hero," as the puppy had become known to her.

Much to everyone's delight, Hero soon recovered, it was really a matter of dehydration and malnutrition that had caused his demise. Both of these matters were quite quickly and easily taken care of and he soon began to grow and flourish in leaps and bounds. Dottie and the Owner were quite happy, in the beginning, to nurse the little Hero back to health, but once he found his feet and his seemingly endless supply of hyper energy, even Dottie began to grow tired of his constant rambunctiousness. Numerous searches in the bush and surrounding areas had not, as yet, yielded even one clue as to the whereabouts of the other puppies. It was only left to hope that they had all found their way to safety.

As Dottie sat in the shade of the little orange tree, which was now growing in spurts and even sported one or two sprays of sweet smelling orange blossom, she began to wonder if life would ever get back to normal. As she sat and ruminated, she heard an almighty CRASH resound from within the apartment and all of a sudden,

Hero came flying outside dragging a white, lacy tablecloth in his now iron like jaws. Dottie just stared at him in alarm, she didn't even want to imagine what he could have demolished or what terrible mischief he had perpetrated! A look passed between the two canines, one of disdain on Dottie's part and one of challenge on the part of Hero. Dottie knew then and there that the puppy had to go, and just at that very moment she heard a heart felt wail come from her Owner inside the apartment, "That puppy has to go!!"

Of course, unmitigated care and attention was given to the task of finding a suitable home for Hero. Both Dottie and the Owner wanted their little charge to grow up happy and healthy, and most of all, loved. Finally they found him the perfect place, a total animal lover, who was already the proud Mama of three dogs and two cats. She, on hearing the story of how Hero had been discovered and saved, was more than happy to make room for one more friend in her already hectic household. That having been accomplished to the satisfaction of all concerned, Dottie and her Owner settled once more to a less frenetic way of life, one they much preferred and certainly appreciated!

CHAPTER NINE

After Hero had been packed off to his new home, a sense of peace and harmony seemed to descend on Dottie. For quite a while she was content to divide her time between lying in the back yard letting the sun bake her to a crisp, and the breeze ruffle her fur, and making sorties into the bush to make absolutely sure that there was not even a remote trace of Hero's family. Soon, however, she began to get just a little bit bored with the complacent way of life that she had slipped into. She found that her thoughts kept wandering more frequently to past adventures and escapades. She often woke from a dream with her adrenalin pumping and her legs twitching with excitement. Dottie discovered that she missed these sensations. She was definitely overdue for another adventure, and the opportunity came much more quickly than even she could have imagined!

It was now June, and the heat was almost unbearable, only alleviated by the very occasional heavy downpour of summer rain, that barely quenched the arid earth and steamed on the baking roads. It was the season of bush fires, fires that were generally ignited by the glare of the sun on pieces of broken glass, beer bottles and other refuse that had been tossed irresponsibly into the bush from passing cars. It seemed as if no sooner had one area of bush burst into flame, than it spread with incredible speed to the next. The barely apparent breeze served only to fan the flames to even greater heights. Firemen were loathe to waste precious water if the fire was not endangering life or property, and so fires often raged unchecked for days. The Island would be completely engulfed in the acrid, lung stinging smoke. For days after the fires had burned out, a pall of grey smoke would hang overhead, serving as a dismal reminder of people's carelessness.

Dottie had decided to do one more, probably last and final check that Hero's family were not lurking in some, hitherto unexplored ,area of the bush. As she made her way through the thick undergrowth she could feel the hard, cracked earth under her feet and the brittle, razor sharp leaves and branches that stabbed at her sides, as she forced her way deeper into the bush. Shards of sunlight glinted on the half buried remnants of broken bottles and glass containers. The whole bush seemed leached of verdure, as though all softness and moisture had been sucked dry by the merciless sun, glaring down out of the sky. The dust prickled her eyes and nose and coated her throat with a bitter grittiness. She felt so lethargic, as though her body was weighted down and her paws had suddenly become lead weights. Every step was an effort of will, every turn of her head a test of endurance. Beads of sweat broke out all over her body and within seconds she was soaked, her fur slicked and sleek to her back. As she turned around to retrace her steps, a flash of light reflected in the corner of her eye and she turned sharply towards it. She could not see anything that could have caused the flash and she stood motionless on the spot, senses straining to catch any hint of movement or light. As she stood mesmerised by the stillness, she felt as though she was in a vacuum, where even time was standing still. As if in slow motion, she turned her head and once again saw the flash of light, it was caused by the sun reflecting on some object that lay on the ground just ahead of her. Dottie started towards it, curious to know what it could be. As she drew nearer she saw that it was a pair of broken spectacles lying twisted on the ground, one lens was shattered and the other still intact. It was this lens that was catching the glare of the sun, and as she looked at it, the sun hit the lens again and

As she drew nearer, she saw that
it was a pair of broken spectacles
lying twisted on the ground.

she was completely dazzled for a moment. When she opened her eyes she saw a thin plume of smoke spiralling upwards from the patch of earth. She came to life with a jolt as she realised that something bad was happening, and as she pulled back in alarm, the first flames crackled and spit into life. Right under Dottie's nose flames were bursting into existence, and before she could even react, runnels of blue flame were licking up the trees and running along the branches as everything crackled and popped like a breakfast cereal. The bush was like a giant tinder box just waiting for a spark to ignite its fury. Within seconds Dottie was completely surrounded by flames that hissed and flickered like demented animals. A primal, naked fear gripped Dottie, she was rooted to the spot in sheer terror. She could feel the intense, soul numbing heat of the raging fire against her face and body, and as she stood hypnotised for a moment, her mind was filled with fascination and awe. It was only when she realised that her fur was on fire and the sickly, sweet smell made her stomach lurch in protest, that she came to her senses and her instincts took over. She frantically looked around her for a way out, but it seemed at first that all exits were blocked by the now blazing fire. Dottie began running in circles, trying desperately to find a way out of the inferno, she narrowly escaped a huge, blazing branch as it crashed to the ground in front of her. She saw that it had left a gaping hole in the foliage where it had detached itself. Without taking a breath, Dottie leapt through the gap. Before she had even made landfall on the other side, she was already racing ahead, dodging flames and burning debris, her fur now totally on fire, smoke streaking behind her as she ran.

The heat was so intense that Dottie felt sure that she would spontaneously combust at any moment. It was the sheer will to survive that kept her going, pictures of her Owner and her Boy flashed through her head as she faltered and almost went down. Her throat and eyes were now so raw that the pain was unbearable and became one with the even greater pain of burning flesh.

Dottie was now navigating by pure instinct, she could not see or hear anything. She just knew that she had to keep going or die in the attempt!

CHAPTER TEN

As Dottie surged forward in an all out attempt to escape, she gradually became aware of a persistent, jarring sound that seemed to grow louder and more insistent as she pushed her way towards it. Something about the sound was deeply familiar and it resonated in the recesses of her subliminal memory and became as a beacon guiding her home. It was not until she finally streaked out into the clearing that she realised exactly what the sound was. As ice cold, life affirming water blasted her, taking her breath away and almost knocking her off her feet, Dottie saw that her saviours were none other than that stalwart company of men whose mascot had been the Dalmatian dog for generations. Several firemen were spraying jets of water into the flames and as the wailing siren subsided with a groan, Dottie heard her name being called, and as her Owner ran towards her, Dottie fell at her feet in a dead faint.

Over the weeks that followed, as Dottie lay uncomfortably recovering on her bed of soft, cotton sheets, she began to realise what a fortunate dog she really was. She had had so many narrow escapes in her two years of life, probably more adventures already than the average dog experienced in a lifetime! Dottie had no complaints of course, apart from the present discomfort of third degree burns, which brought her sharply to her senses every time she moved even slightly. She knew deep down that everyone has to bear the consequences of their actions, however painful they may be! To Dottie, a life of adventure and excitement, with all the incumbent dangers, was preferable to the boring ,sedentary life that so many dogs of her calibre lead. Dottie personally knew many pedigree dogs who lay around all day being primped and pampered, and growing fatter by the minute! The highlight of their day being the never ending supply of delicacies and treats that their Owners pressed upon them! Not that Dottie didn't enjoy the odd treat now and then, her favourites were those bone-shaped, crunchy dog biscuits that her Owner gave her when she had been extra helpful or cooperative. However, there was a time and place for everything and right now, Dottie was quite enjoying the extra attention that her latest exploits had generated. Her photograph had appeared in the local newspaper under the blaring headline, "DARING DALMATIAN NARROWLY ESCAPES INFERNO!!" She just wished she hadn't looked quite so burnt and frazzled in the otherwise extremely flattering coverage of her adventure.

As the days went by, each one found Dottie feeling just a little better, and before too long she was up and about and gingerly making her way around her property. She still felt stiff and sore, but was healing amazingly well. Of course, the areas where she had been burnt, mostly along her sides and flank, were still very pink and completely without fur. Putting vanity aside, she was just glad to be on her feet again. After all, fur would grow again eventually and she might even find that she had a few more spots than before, anything was possible!!

CHAPTER ELEVEN

Dottie found that she had now been confined to the yard. The side gate, which had hitherto been so easy to unlatch, was, she discovered, securely locked with a brand new, shiny padlock! At first she was extremely put out by this discovery and barked angrily at it. When she realised that there was no way around it, she began to howl in frustration. The Owner laughed heartily when she saw what the problem was," It's for your own good Dottie, you are far too adventurous. You need to keep a low profile for a while until those burns are completely healed. We cannot risk getting them infected, so, sorry but the gate must remain locked, for the time being at least!" With that she went inside and left Dottie gazing futilely at the locked gate.

Dottie slumped down, with a tremendous sigh, under the orange tree. Sometimes life just didn't seem fair! She was hardly going to wander off into the bush again any time soon. The whole area was a charred, burnt out mass, nothing had escaped those hungry flames and it had taken the Fire Brigade several hours to completely extinguish the fire. Surprisingly enough, small, green shoots had already begun to push their way through the scorched earth, and before too long, the bush would be a lush green again. Mother Nature is wonderful, thought Dottie, not even a trauma such as that could hinder her progress.

She lay feeling bored and hard done to and was just on the point of dropping off to sleep when the back door opened and there stood her Boy!! Dottie thought she must be either hallucinating or already asleep and dreaming!! She jumped to her feet, barely wincing as the newly healed burns pulled sharply and painfully. The two collided in an embrace as he fell to his knees and she ran full pelt into his arms. They rolled and scrambled in the grass, until the Boy said,"Oops, we'd better take it easy on those burns Dot, we don't want to make them any worse than they are, do we?" Dottie, in that moment really didn't care, she was so totally happy to see him. "How does a dip in the ocean sound?" he asked with a smile in his voice. Dottie raced him to the door, where he clipped on her leash, and the two of them set off for their most favourite place of all, the place where each could truly be free.

The next two months went by in a blur of happiness for Dottie. She was permanently on the go, barely even finding time to catch a quick nap under the orange tree, before the Boy was calling her to go somewhere with him.

Dottie sitting upright in the passenger seat, eyes forward, ready for off.

One Sunday, the Boy took Dottie down to the East End of the Island with him. He wanted to take a look at a boat that he heard had been grounded on a beach several miles from Freeport, towards the East End of Grand Bahama Island. They climbed into his jeep, Dottie sitting upright in the passenger seat, eyes forward, ready for off, the Boy making last minute adjustments to radio, seat belt and seat inclination. When everything was just so, they set off. The sky was a brilliant shade of blue, with clouds like cotton wool balls floating across the horizon.

The road to East End was long and monotonous, flanked as it was by row upon row of unwavering Yellow Pine trees, that stood tall and spindly on either side of the road, like gangly sentinels. The road, although now paved, had once been little more than a glorified mud track, pounded flat by the steady stream of East bound traffic over the years. Today, however, the road lay ahead smooth and straight and the sun squinted through the trunks of the Pines, casting shadows across the asphalt that resembled bars on a prison door. The Boy had his windows down and his music pumped up so that the jeep shook and rattled with every base chord. As the wind rushed into their faces and the music filled their ears, Dottie and the Boy felt the old familiar tug of excitement on their heart strings, and with a smile of satisfaction they set off once more on the road to adventure!

Fifty minutes later, they swerved to a halt in a shower of sand, in front of a rickety, wooden shack, that had been garishly painted in vibrant shades of red, yellow and green. On the outside stood several tables fashioned from planks of wood bound together with ropes, and numerous twine bobbins that seemed to serve as seats. The wooden bobbins had been washed clean by the summer rain and worn smooth by the rhythm of the ocean waves. In the rear of the shack stood an ancient, hand made barbecue grill, belching out smoke and filling the air with mouth watering smells of chicken and roast conch.

The Boy jumped out of the jeep and went inside to ask directions as to the whereabouts of the grounded boat.

Dottie slowly climbed out of the jeep and shook herself. She stretched languidly, her paws making runnels in the damp sand. She lay flat on her stomach, letting the sun warm her back, the sea soaked sand cool her front, and the sweet smell of cooking food tease her nostrils. The seagulls screamed noisily overhead, as they swooped close to the empty tables, hoping to find some tasty tidbit left by a lunching local. Dottie followed their antics out of the corners of her eyes. She kept her head perfectly still, without the slightest trace of movement, while her eye balls rotated in all directions, never letting them out of her sight. Too soon they were lulled into a false sense of security by the immobile dog. They began to land on tables in the immediate vicinity and even on the sand at her feet! Dottie's body vibrated with anticipation as she readied herself for exactly the Right Moment.

As the fat, beady eyed, sharp beaked birds waddled closer, Dottie arched her back, ready to spring. One of the gulls seemed to sense something as he ruffled his feathers skittishly, ready for flight. Dottie leapt into the air, amid a flock of air bourne birds, becoming one with them in their quest to reach the sky. Her soaring grace matched theirs for a few brief seconds, before gravity stepped in, and she fell to earth, her legs still pumping. Dottie raced along the beach, barking angrily at the flock of gulls above her, who screeched mockingly at her defeat.

The Boy was now coming back, with two other people in tow. They were all talking earnestly and Dottie caught the word "boat" mentioned repeatedly. They all took off along the beach, with Dottie following at her own pace.

There were several large rock formations at intervals along the beach, and Dottie discovered that many of them housed rock pools that were teeming with life. She poked her head into the cool, murky water and felt tiny fish and other sea creatures tickle her face. She snapped half heartedly at them, often sneezing and coughing as she inhaled the salty sea water!

After a while she came across a pool that was deeper and bigger than any of the others and so she decided to stay there and cool her heels for a while. She stepped into the pool and stood surveying the horizon and glancing from time to time in the direction that the Boy had gone. She took pleasure in splashing the surface of the water with her paw and watching the shoals of tiny fish dart away from her. Soon she slipped down into a sitting position, the water chilling her sides pleasantly, her eyes began to close as she felt herself totally relax. Suddenly the peaceful scene was shattered as Dottie leapt to her feet with a cry of anguish, she jumped out of the little pool shaking her back leg vigorously and squealing with pain. She howled and howled, the whole time frantically trying to rid her back leg of something that was clinging on to her for dear life, and had no intention of letting go!! The Boy came running over the sand, his feet sinking in almost to his knees, as he tried to get to her as quickly as he could. He grabbed on to her as she ran in circles in a last ditch attempt to free herself from the agonising pain in her back leg. The Boy held her in a tight grip as he took her leg into his hand to see what was causing her so much distress. There, attached firmly to her paw, was the largest Hermit Crab that the Boy had ever seen! It's huge pincers were firmly embedded in Dottie's flesh! The Boy gasped and quickly tried to force the crab to loosen its hold on Dottie. The pincers remained firmly in position. The Boy concentrated his efforts on getting Dottie to calm down and keep still for a moment. Then he reached into the pool and found a large, solid piece of rock. He held Dottie's leg firmly in his left hand, forcing her to stand behind him, as he took the rock in his right hand and with one, short, sharp, forceful blow, he sent the crab, complete with shell, flying through the air and back into the pool with a loud plop!! Dottie began licking her paw ferociously, it felt so much better now that the dreadful thing had let go of her. She glanced nervously into the pool, but was relieved to note that the creature was no where in sight!

They all took off along the beach with
Dottie following at her own pace.

After the hullabaloo had died down, Dottie and her Boy shared a piece of chicken, fresh from the grill, the Boy letting Dottie have all her favourite, juicy parts and soon the incident was almost forgotten. However, Dottie had made a mental note, to never, ever go anywhere near a rock pool again, no matter how inviting!!!

The journey back was uneventful, much to Dottie's relief ,she had had enough adventure for one day!! Soon the Boy would be leaving her again and life would take on the familiar pattern of getting on with things until it was time for him to return. Dottie could only dream of the day when he would be back for good and they could have new, and hitherto unimagined, adventures together for ever and ever!!! In the meantime she was just content to be at his side as they made their way back home.

THE END. [for now!!!!]

Dottie, the Spottie Dalmatian dog
dreaming of the day when they would
have new, and hitherto unimagined
adventures together for ever and ever!

Printed in the United States
40446LVS00002B